Elspeth Hart
and the
School for Show-offs

For Mum and Dad, of course – SF
For Amy, Eliza and Martha x – JB

STRIPES PUBLISHING
An imprint of Little Tiger Press
1 The Coda Centre, 189 Munster Road,
London SW6 6AW

A paperback original
First published in Great Britain in 2015

ISBN: 978-1-84715-595-5

Printed and bound in the UK.

10 9 8 7 6 5 4 3 2 1

Elspeth Hart
and the
School for Show-offs

Sarah Forbes

Illustrated by James Brown

stripes

Miss Crabb

Gladys Goulash

Professor Bombast

Madame Chi-chi

Madame Stringy

Rory
Snitter

Tatiana
Firensky

Esmerelda
Higginsbot

Tim
Fitzgibbons

Octavia
Ornamento

1
Another Horrible Tuesday

It was three o'clock on a Tuesday, and Miss Crabb was picking her nose. She was digging her long, pointy finger right inside her nostril and pulling out the most awful strings of green snot.

Elspeth Hart was staring at her in horror. She didn't want to watch, but she couldn't help it.

"Gah! What are you staring at, you
little ratbag?" shouted Miss Crabb, when
she realized Elspeth was watching. "Can't
a body pick her own nostrils in peace?
Gerroff down to the cellars and sweep up the
mouse droppings! I might need them as an
ingredient in the stew I'm making. Get to it!"

Elspeth hurried off. She had only lived
with Miss Crabb for a year, but she already
knew not to cross her. Miss Crabb was

Elspeth's aunt. She had a nasty temper and a never-ending list of disgusting chores she could make Elspeth do.

Elspeth and Miss Crabb didn't live in a house like most people. They lived in a boarding school. Miss Crabb was the Chief Cook at the school and she lived in a very small attic right at the top of the building. So when Elspeth moved in, there wasn't much space for her. She had to sleep in a wardrobe.

Yes, dear reader – a wardrobe! It doesn't seem very fair to me, either. That was bad enough, but the school itself was even worse. It was a drama school called the Pandora Pants School for Show-offs and it was a dreadful place. You could only study there if you were really, really good at showing off, or your parents were very rich.

Hundreds and hundreds of film stars, TV stars, people in adverts – they had all been to the Pandora Pants School for Show-offs, once upon a time. And some of the students were nastier than a mouthful of mouldy cabbage.

The Pandora Pants School for Show-offs was not a place you would want to visit. Ever. Unless you, dear reader, are a show-off. Are you?

I thought not. And nor was Elspeth Hart.

Elspeth Hart was a bit shorter than you are, and a bit shyer than you are. She had green eyes and fuzzy dark hair that was hard to control. She had lived a normal life until she was ten, when her parents disappeared in a flood and were never seen again. That was when she had come to live with Miss Crabb.

"More mouse droppings," Elspeth muttered, as she stepped into the dark cellar. "I can't believe she gets away with putting them in the food. Evil old woman."

She moved sideways in the dark, feeling around for the light switch, and bashed her knee hard against the wall. Tears came to her eyes, but Elspeth blinked them away.

She switched on the light, looked around the stinky, dripping cellar and started sweeping very slowly. Elspeth could hear Miss Crabb upstairs, crashing and banging around the kitchen in a rage, and she was in no hurry to go back.

"STUPID LITTLE VARMINTS!" Miss Crabb was shouting. "I CAN'T BELIEVE I HAVE TO COOK FOR THESE STUPID LITTLE VARMINTS!"

There was the sound of smashing glass.

Miss Crabb hated
the children at
the Pandora
Pants School for
Show-offs. She
hated Elspeth, too.
And if Miss Crabb
met you, dear reader,
I am afraid that
she would hate
you, no matter
how friendly you
are. Children
were Miss
Crabb's sworn
enemies, and she
did everything she could to
make poor Elspeth's life a misery.
When Elspeth came to live with her,

Miss Crabb instantly put her to work in the filthiest, stickiest, darkest corner of the kitchen and gave her all sorts of other horrible jobs around the school. Elspeth never complained. As you know, she was quite a bit shyer than you are, and besides, she had been brought up to be very polite. So poor Elspeth had to scrub pots and shoo away cockroaches and watch Miss Crabb make the most disgusting school dinners in the world.

If you've ever tried to keep your head down in a horrible situation, dear reader, you can imagine how poor Elspeth felt. But what Elspeth didn't know, as she swept up hundreds of mouse droppings in a creepy dark cellar, was that things were about to change.

2
Other Creepy Dark Places

The next morning, Elspeth woke up early and lay in her wardrobe, wishing she was anywhere else but the Pandora Pants School for Show-offs. She had a crick in her neck and she could feel an ant crawling along her foot. She closed her eyes again and tried to remember what her mum and dad looked like. It was no use. Elspeth couldn't even remember the flood that had washed away her parents. She had gone to sleep one night and, when she woke up, Miss Crabb was standing over her, telling her that the Pandora Pants School for Show-offs was her new home.

"I hate this place!" Elspeth whispered to herself. She flicked the ant off her foot and thought about running away.

She dreamed of running away all the time. But the school was at the end of a deserted road, with nothing else around as far as the eye could see. Elspeth didn't know what was out there, but she knew she was many, many miles from anyone who could help her.

Just as Elspeth was about to get up, she heard a dreadful cracking and creaking noise.

Elspeth peered out of her wardrobe and saw Miss Crabb doing her morning aerobics. She was wearing a moth-eaten leotard and leopard-print leggings. Her hair stood out in a frizzy halo and she hadn't put in her false teeth yet. Elspeth looked on in horror as Miss Crabb did a series of high kicks. One of her gnarly yellow feet nearly kicked Elspeth in the face.

And the very worst thing was the smell. Miss Crabb always let out a series of disgusting farts when she was exercising.

Elspeth held her breath and made a run for the bathroom. She turned on the taps and filled up the massive old-fashioned bathtub. There was never enough hot water, but sometimes Elspeth would lie in there for ages, dreaming that the bathtub would fly away and she would never have to scrub another pot again. Or that her parents would magically come back and take her home. Or that Miss Crabb would start doing jigsaws instead of aerobics.

Sadly, none of Elspeth's dreams ever came true. No one had come to rescue Elspeth and, to make matters worse, Elspeth was NEVER ALLOWED OUTSIDE. Never ever.

Can you imagine never being allowed outside, dear reader – even when the sun is shining and being indoors makes you feel all stuffy and wriggly?

"Miss Crabb, why can't I go and play outside?" Elspeth had asked in her first week at the school. The show-offs were running around the massive overgrown gardens. It all looked like great fun, but Elspeth was stuck indoors.

"You ain't allowed out for your own good," said Miss Crabb, who was chopping up rats' tails for a soup. "I'm sorry to break it to you, but you are allergic to fresh air."

"What?" Elspeth was suspicious. "I'm not allergic to fresh air. Nobody is allergic to fresh air."

Miss Crabb stabbed the knife into the chopping board so hard that it stuck there,

quivering. She gave Elspeth a
most terrifying glare.

"Well, *you* are,"
she said. She gave an
angry sniff. "And
unless you want to
drop dead on the
spot, I suggest you

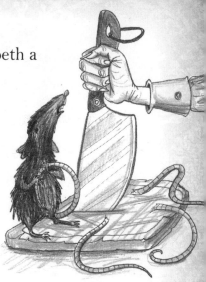

keep yourself inside the school premises at
all times."

"But, Miss Crabb, I'm sure I used to
play outside…" Elspeth paused. Could she
remember playing outside? Little memories
would flash into her head from time to time,
but none of them were very clear. "I mean,
I think I did. I can't quite remember…"
Elspeth trailed off.

"It's the flood," Miss Crabb said, turning
back to her chopping board. "It affected

your memory, so you'll just have to believe me." She started chopping again, and Elspeth stared at her in confusion.

"Get on with your work, child!" Miss Crabb hissed.

All in all, dear reader, it was a pretty miserable life, and there was just one person Elspeth could trust. Her only friend in the whole school. In fact, right now, her only friend in the whole world.

3
Elspeth's Only Friend in the Whole World

He was a secret friend. His name was Rory Snitter and although he was a pupil at the Pandora Pants School for Show-offs, he wasn't a very good show-off. In fact, Rory was a bit of a crybaby, but he was the only pupil who ever smiled at Elspeth. One day he'd shown Elspeth a secret hiding place when Miss Crabb was chasing her with a rolling pin. The pair had been friends ever since, and they used the same secret hiding place to meet every morning.

Elspeth tiptoed through the Great Grand Hall. The hall had a sweeping staircase and a magnificent log fire. At one end was a massive portrait of Pandora Pants, the woman who had started the school. She was pouting in the picture and wearing a hideous green ballgown. Elspeth shuddered when she went past it. She shuddered again when she had to walk over the huge tiger-skin rug. Professor Bombast, the headmaster, claimed he liked to shoot things (when he wasn't busy teaching in a very LOUD VOICE). This meant there were also stuffed owls and deer antlers hanging on the walls.

Elspeth crept towards the theatre at the

back of the building, where the show-offs staged their impressive school shows. Under the stage was the perfect place to meet Rory in secret.

"So Crabb was doing her aerobics again? Yuck!" Rory said when Elspeth crawled into their hiding place, looking green.

Rory could tell immediately that Miss Crabb's farts had been extra bad that morning.

"She is *so* disgusting," Elspeth hissed. "I can't stand it! It's OK for you, at least your parents are coming to get you at the end of term."

"I suppose." Rory wrinkled up his nose. "Won't exactly be exciting, though. They just go off on holidays all the time and leave me with the butler. He's no fun."

"Well, it sounds a lot better than being

stuck here," said Elspeth.

"Yeah, I guess so." Rory sighed. "I just found out I've been put in Remedial Tap Dancing this term. I hate it. Just because I'm not as good as Tim Fitzgibbons. He's won awards for it and everything!"

Elspeth looked at her friend in his smart shoes and blazer, and felt sorry for him. Rory's hair was neatly combed, and he had a pen clipped to his shirt pocket as usual.

Elspeth knew he worked hard at school, but he could never compete with the other show-offs.

Instead of learning how to spell and do maths, the show-offs were taught things like Showing Off in Public, Attention Seeking in General, Creating a Scene, Getting Your Own Way and Extreme Boasting. If you can think of the most annoying person in your class, dear reader, and then multiply them by a million, that will give you an idea of what the show-offs were like.

Elspeth and Rory were quiet for a moment while Rory's pet lizard, Lazlo, crawled up and down his arm. Apart from Elspeth, Lazlo the lizard was Rory's best friend. Lazlo looked cute, but he had a vicious bite and a nasty temper, too.

Last year, one of the show-offs had stuffed Lazlo down the back of Professor Bombast's trousers as part of a magic trick in the school show. Professor Bombast had leaped and bounced and shrieked, and everyone agreed it was the best thing they'd seen in ages.

Elspeth put out a hand to pat Lazlo, then hesitated. She'd seen how sharp his pointy little teeth were.

"What was your house like?" Rory asked suddenly. "When you lived with your mum and dad?"

Elspeth paused. She screwed up her eyes and tried to remember.

"I know we lived in a flat above my parents' sweet shop in a place called Skipping Hopton," she said. "I can't remember it very clearly, but I think

they made their own sweets. Oh, wait
– I remember one thing! There was an
enormous candyfloss machine with a glass
cover, almost as tall as me!"

Elspeth tried, but she couldn't remember
anything else. It made her sad. She
couldn't picture her parents' faces, but she
remembered how it felt to hug her mum. It
was a very fuzzy memory, but when Elspeth
thought of her, she remembered the smell
of sugar and cinammon. She didn't tell Rory
that, though. She didn't want to get upset.

"It sounds like a cool place to live! I'd
LOVE to live above a sweet shop," Rory
said. "Do you have any photos?" Then
he stopped and looked serious. "Sorry,
Elspeth," he said. "Stupid question. I know
you don't have any of your things with you."

All Elspeth Hart had in the world were

the clothes she had been wearing when
she was rescued from the flood. Just her
threadbare purple dress and purple trainers.
Elspeth often wished she had new clothes,
but she would never part with her trainers.
Her dad had helped her decorate them with
swirly designs and stars using a marker pen.
No matter how often the show-offs laughed
at them, Elspeth still loved them.

"That's OK, don't feel bad," Elspeth said,
fiddling with the laces on her trainers. They
were starting to pinch her feet.

Just then the bell shrilled.

"We'd better go," Elspeth said, jumping up. She made a face. "I hope I can avoid Tatiana Firensky today."

Tatiana Firensky was the very worst of the show-offs. Her father owned the Firensky Glue Company, and Tatiana was spoiled rotten. She had long shiny blonde hair, sharp fingernails and a mean temper, and she was very good at getting her own way. Tatiana had been horrible to Elspeth ever since she had arrived at the school.

Rory nodded. "Good luck!" he hissed over his shoulder, as he tucked Lazlo into his pocket and hurried off to his first class.

Elspeth moved quickly and quietly towards the stairs. She was an expert at making herself invisible – flattening herself against the corridor wall when Tatiana was coming towards her, or walking behind Tim Fitzgibbons, who was the tallest boy in the school.

Elspeth had learned that being almost invisible was the best way to survive in the Pandora Pants School for Show-offs.

4
Almost Invisible ...
But Not Quite

Cleaning the school took Elspeth ages, because there were so many floors in the Pandora Pants School for Show-offs. At the very top of the school, as you know, were Miss Crabb's living quarters. On the floors below were the classrooms and dormitories. Elspeth always ended up with spiders in her hair when she had to do the cleaning. No matter how hard she tried to clean, the rooms always seemed musty and cobwebby. But delicious sounds could be heard floating up from where Madame Stringy, the music teacher, was teaching violin to the finest students.

"Gotcha," Elspeth muttered, as she plucked a large spider from her messy hair and placed it in a little box she carried in her pocket. Tatiana Firensky hated spiders. Elspeth had worked out that if Tatiana caused her any trouble, releasing a big spider would send her into instant hysterics, giving Elspeth a chance to escape. She smiled at the thought of it. But as she got on with her cleaning, Elspeth heard a sharp tapping sound coming from the dance studio next door.

Elspeth froze. She was sure the school was haunted. Could it be a ghost? She moved slowly towards the door and stepped into the corridor.

Please don't be a ghost, please don't be a ghost, Elspeth thought.

She held her breath and tiptoed along the corridor, then she peeked around the door and sighed in relief. It was only Tim Fitzgibbons practising his tap dancing.

Tim Fitzgibbons was not only the tallest boy in the school, he was also the best looking. He was an expert in ballet, tap, Irish dancing, kickboxing, break-dancing and the hokey-cokey.

"Hello!" Tim said in a loud-but-friendly voice. "Come to learn a few skills, have you?"

He did a very fancy move as he said this, tapping so quickly his feet were a blur. "Professor Bombast said I could spend the morning rehearsing in here. Hey, do you think my hair looks OK?"

Tim Fitzgibbons ran a hand through his perfect hair. He looked worried. "I can't work out if I'm more handsome with it swept to the left side —" he moved his hair over to one side — "or the right…"

Elspeth tried not to laugh. She couldn't believe how much the show-offs worried about their hair. Especially the boys.

"I think your hair looks absolutely perfect," Elspeth replied.

"Wow, thanks!" Tim Fitzgibbons took a closer look in the mirror on the wall. "You're right, it *is* perfect! I look AMAZING!"

"It's so much better than anyone else's hair," Elspeth said. She tried to sound impressed. Could Tim Fitzgibbons be her friend? Having a popular show-off as a friend in the school might make things much easier. Then she felt like a bit of a fake. *Pretending to be someone's friend is never a good idea*, she thought.

"I'd better go," she said, picking up her broom and cleaning bucket.

"Bye, then!" shouted Tim cheerfully. He was still rearranging his hair when Elspeth left.

She went down to the next floor to start on the classrooms (which looked a bit like your classroom, dear reader, except the chairs were fancy gold ones with soft velvet seats).

She swept up a load of chocolate-bar wrappers. Professor Bombast often liked a snack in the middle of lessons. As usual, there was a half-eaten Chump bar sitting on the desk. Elspeth grabbed it and munched it down quickly. She was always hungry because she hardly ever managed to eat the disgusting food Miss Crabb cooked – she knew what went into it, and it was vile.

Elspeth cleaned all the other floors in the school, finishing with the Great Grand

Hall. Finally, she made her way down to the nasty mouse-infested cellar to put away her cleaning things. When she went in she had to hold her nose. The cellar smelled even worse than usual, which meant that Miss Crabb's assistant, Gladys Goulash, must have been in there recently. Gladys Goulash was even dirtier than Miss Crabb. She only took a bath once a year, just before the annual Look at Us! show.

Elspeth raced back up the stairs and breathed in clean air in relief. Even though she'd had to do loads of horrible work, it hadn't been a bad day at all so far. She hadn't seen evil Tatiana Firensky once.

But unfortunately for Elspeth, Tatiana Firensky had seen HER.

5
And Tatiana Firensky Was Not Happy

Tatiana Firensky was having a tantrum.
If you were having a tantrum, dear reader,
other people would probably know all about
it. You might turn pink or get a bit spluttery,
or perhaps, if you were feeling brave, you
might do a bit of shouting. But Tatiana's
tantrums were not like anyone else's.

On the surface, she stayed very, very

calm and kept a fixed smile on her pretty mouth. But inside she was scheming and plotting and coming up with all kinds of evil plans.

Tatiana was with her two best friends, Octavia Ornamento and Esmerelda Higginsbot, in the Great Grand Hall. She was perched on the best chair she could find, which looked a bit like a throne. Octavia was studying her face in a mirror. Esmerelda was doing the splits and plaiting her long glossy hair at the same time.

Tatiana cleared her throat, and Octavia and Esmerelda jumped to attention.

"I have had quite enough," Tatiana began in her high, clear voice. "I have had enough of that little snot rag poking around our classrooms, dirtying our books with her filthy thumbs."

"Do you mean Professor Bombast?" asked Octavia Ornamento, her blue eyes wide. Octavia was not a very bright girl.

"She means Elspeth Hart," Esmerelda hissed out of the corner of her mouth.

"Oh." Octavia's eyelashes fluttered as she tried to process this information in her slow-moving brain. "Yes. What are we going to do about her?"

"That," said Tatiana from behind gritted teeth, "is why I have called you both here, you useless idiot. We are going to have to stop her in her tracks. I saw her spying on Tim Fitzgibbons earlier. When he was trying to rehearse! Who does she think she is? I wanted to spy on him and she BEAT ME TO IT!"

"I saw her sneaking into the library last week," said Esmerelda. "I thought she was supposed to be a kitchen assistant. She's obviously got ideas above her station."

"I think," said Tatiana, her mouth curling into an evil smile, "that if the little ratbag imagines she can be one of us, we will have to teach her otherwise!" She rapped her long fingernails on the edge of the chair. "And I've got the perfect plan. We'll set a trap in that stinking library. Something that she can't resist. We'll give her such a fright that she'll run away and never come back ever again!"

Esmerelda gave a little snort, then darted her eyes towards Tatiana to check if she was allowed to laugh. Tatiana stared back at her sternly, then broke into chilling cackles. Octavia joined in, although she still didn't have a clue what was going on.

Just then Madame Chi-chi appeared, wearing an enormous purple cloak and even more lipstick than usual. "You are all-a supposed-a to be in my Creating a Scene-a class!" she shouted. "Come at once-a!" She hauled Esmerelda and Octavia up by their ears. But she didn't dare touch Tatiana Firensky. None of the teachers did.

Tatiana's father was so important that she could have anyone fired in a flash. She had one of the caretakers sacked last year after he polished the floor and put a rug down in the Great Grand Hall, causing Tatiana to skid across the hall and fall on her bottom.

Tatiana had simply pulled herself to her feet, given everyone a fearsome look and phoned her father, asking him to file an Official Filthy Rich Complaint on special pink paper. Very soon after, the caretaker disappeared and was never seen again. Nobody messed with Tatiana Firensky. You could never tell when she might strike.

6
Tatiana Strikes!

The next day, it was Elspeth's job to help out in the classrooms. She had to be in Professor Bombast's class first thing, but she hid under the stage until the very last minute and then sprinted up the stairs when the bell rang. This meant the show-offs had less time to pick on her. It also meant Elspeth had pink cheeks and stickyuppy hair from racing to the classroom. But as you know, dear reader, there are much more important things in life than having perfect hair.

"Late again, you little varmint!" shrilled Miss Crabb from the kitchen, lobbing a rotten potato at Elspeth as she passed.

Elspeth ducked out of the way just in time and kept running. In her dirty old dress, she stood out among all the show-offs strolling down the corridors in their fancy school uniform. The uniform even had a school crest on the blazer, which was a picture of some frilly pants.

Elspeth whirled into the classroom so fast she tripped on a bit of sticking-up carpet, making all the show-offs point and laugh.

"Stupid carpet!" Elspeth muttered under

her breath, picking herself up. The carpet looked expensive, but it hadn't been stuck down properly, because Professor Bombast wanted to save money.

The whole school was the same. The bits on display, like the Great Grand Hall and the theatre, were beautiful and expensive-looking. That was so the show-offs' rich parents would be dazzled when they came to visit. But behind the scenes, the showers were full of insects, the kitchens were disgusting and the dormitories were poky and cold. None of the show-offs complained though, because they were all so desperate to be famous.

"Aha! THERE YOU ARE!" shouted Professor Bombast, striding towards Elspeth. He was a very tall man, almost twice the height of Elspeth, and about one and a half times the height of you, dear reader. Professor Bombast had a shock of curly-wurly black hair and he didn't like to sit still even for a moment. His pet pit bull, Cutie-pie, didn't like to sit still, either. He trotted along at Professor Bombast's ankles wherever he went.

Like the school, Professor Bombast was a fake. He wasn't really a professor at all. He had just bought a certificate online saying he was.

"HAND OUT THESE ESSAYS, WILL YOU, ELSPETH?" he boomed.

Elspeth nodded and went over to take the pile of papers Professor Bombast was waving at her.

None of the show-offs paid any attention. Two of them were practising a ballet scene from *The Nutcracker*. One was crying because he thought a stuffed owl was staring at him. And three of them had started acting out scenes from *Mary Poppins* in a corner of the classroom. They were all making a terrible noise trying to outdo each other.

"PAY ATTENTION!" shouted Professor Bombast.

He marched around the children, giving them all a flick on the ear as he passed.

They were so shocked that they settled down immediately, although there was a lot of quiet sniffling as Elspeth gave out the papers.

There was hardly any homework at the Pandora Pants School for Show-offs, but everyone had to write one essay a year. The topic was always "Why Being Famous Is the Best Thing Ever".

Elspeth handed Esmerelda Higginsbot her essay. Esmerelda glanced at her mark and didn't look happy. She pouted at Tim Fitzgibbons.

Tim Fitzgibbons gave Esmerelda a sympathetic pat on the shoulder, and Tatiana Firensky narrowed her eyes. Elspeth could tell Tatiana got annoyed every time Tim Fitzgibbons was nice to Esmerelda. Elspeth thought it was funny, but she didn't dare laugh. At least, not in front of Tatiana.

"Rory Snitter!" Elspeth called out.

"Here," mumbled Rory, taking his essay from Elspeth without looking at her. They'd got used to pretending they weren't friends in front of the others.

Sometimes Elspeth wondered why Rory was even at the school. He seemed too normal, even a bit shy. She guessed his parents really wanted him to be famous.

"Octavia Ornamento!"

"I am HERE," declared Octavia. She gave a dramatic bow, and snatched the paper quickly from Elspeth's hand.

When Elspeth handed Tatiana Firensky her essay, Tatiana took one look at the paper and shrieked in horror.

"B! I always get As! Always, always, ALWAYS!" Tatiana shrilled. She tossed back her mane of blonde hair and stepped right up to Elspeth, making her stumble backwards into some bookshelves. "I bet *you* had something to do with this," she said. "You've changed my mark!"

Elspeth's stomach tightened into a knot. She was backed up against the shelves with nowhere to go. Before she could duck out of the way, Tatiana gave Elspeth a shove and one of Professor Bombast's biggest, oldest, dustiest books fell from the top shelf and…

GU-DUMPH!

…whacked her hard on the head.

The world went black.

7

And Everything Stayed Black for Five Whole Minutes

When Elspeth woke up, she was lying on the ground with a circle of curious faces peering down at her. Professor Bombast was prodding her on the arm.

"Jolly good, she's still alive!" he said, giving a nervous laugh. "Tatiana, play more … *gently* in future, won't you?"

Tatiana smirked. "Yes, Professor Bombast."

Elspeth felt dizzy. She opened her mouth to speak, but no words came out. Instead, as she lay there waiting for the room to stop spinning, a strange tune ran through her head. She hummed it to herself as Rory Snitter and Tim Fitzgibbons pulled her to her feet.

"One is for sugar, two is for…" Elspeth sang softly. Then she realized the show-offs were watching her and nudging one another.

"Oh dear! Looks like scribbly-shoe girl's lost the plot!" Tatiana said loudly, making all the others snigger.

Elspeth ignored them. She stopped singing out loud and let the tune run through her head instead. Then she tried to look normal before anyone paid more attention to her, but she felt very strange. If you have ever had a bump on the head, dear reader, you will know exactly how she felt.

By lunchtime, the bump on Elspeth's head had become enormous – and it was turning a nasty yellowish-purple. People were staring at her. Some children were even whispering and pointing as she walked past. Elspeth hated it. It was very hard to be invisible when everyone was looking at her and talking about her. And to make things even worse, the mysterious tune was still in her head.

Elspeth wished both the bump and the tune would go away. She rubbed her head nervously as she walked towards Madame Chi-chi's classroom to prepare for the next lesson – Attention Seeking in General. The problem with Madame Chi-chi was that she had violent mood swings. This meant you never knew whether she was going to hug you or throw something at you.

Madame Chi-chi had been a famous actress and one of the biggest show-offs of all time during her career. She had starred in Italy's famous hospital drama,

Mamma Mia, Ouchy Ouchy! There were rumours that once she threw a co-star from a speeding train. Elspeth hoped the rumours weren't true. She knocked timidly on the classroom door.

"Enter!" came Madame Chi-chi's commanding voice. Madame Chi-chi was perched on her desk, which looked exactly like a large gold dressing table. She was applying a thick coat of bright red lipstick.

"Oh. It's you," she said, as Elspeth came in. Madame Chi-chi smacked the lid back on to her lipstick. "I shall need you to place all those chairs in a circle," she continued, "and wipe the board clean. And I hear you've been upsetting the other children, so you can scrape all the old chewing gum off the bottom of the desks."

"I haven't been upsetting anyone!"

Elspeth protested, but Madame Chi-chi wouldn't listen.

Tatiana Firensky did this, Elspeth thought angrily, as she moved the heavy velvet seats around the room. *I haven't done anything to her, and she's turned everyone against me.*

The door flew open just as Elspeth finished wiping the board, and a stream of shouty, pushy show-offs danced into the room.

"Ah! My darling little studentios!" Madame Chi-chi clapped her hands. "Tell me, are you ready to show-a-off-a like-a superstars?!"

"YEEESS!" roared the class.

Tim Fitzgibbons did a graceful pirouette and Octavia Ornamento leaped off her desk.

Just as Elspeth was about to sneak out,

one of the girls in the front row waved at her. Elspeth's heart sank. It was Tatiana Firensky. Again.

"Still wearing those stinky old trainers, Elspeth?" she sneered. "Who actually DRAWS on their own shoes?" Tatiana raised her fountain pen and flicked it towards Elspeth. A massive ink blot appeared on the front of Elspeth's only dress, and all the show-offs shrieked with amusement. Even Tim Fitzgibbons pointed at her and laughed.

"You-a go and clean-a up-a." Madame Chi-chi dismissed her with a wave.

Elspeth closed the door quietly. The bump on her head throbbed as she hurried upstairs.

After cleaning the ink off her hands, Elspeth looked around the stuffy attic bedroom in despair. She didn't have any other clothes to change into. As she dabbed at the mark on her dress with a tissue, Elspeth found herself humming the strange tune again.

What on earth is it? Why can't I remember the rest of the words? Elspeth asked herself. She felt sure the tune was connected to her parents in some way. She tried again to remember what they looked like, and felt very sad. Then she thought about how awful Tatiana and her cronies were being, and she felt extra sad.

"There is *no point* feeling sorry for yourself," she whispered. "That won't help you one bit."

But that strange song made Elspeth think about all the other things she must have forgotten. Her memories of life before arriving at the Pandora Pants School for Show-offs were so hazy. Was the song a sign that she was going to get her memory back? Would she be able to figure out what the song meant? It all seemed rather mysterious.

8

Rather Mysterious Things

That night, Elspeth had strange, wild
dreams. The song ran through her head
over and over, and she could see images
of sticky toffee sauce and gobstoppers
strangely mixed with the mocking sound of
the show-offs laughing at her. She dreamed
that she was in a supermarket with two
vague figures that must have been her

parents, and Miss Crabb was lurking in the background, peering at them from behind a display of baked beans. She woke with a start at six o'clock, sat bolt upright in her wardrobe and listened to the sound of her heart thudding. *One is for sugar,* she caught herself humming.

"That song won't leave me alone," she said to herself. Elspeth touched her forehead. Had the nasty bump on the head helped her remember a song from when she was little?

As Elspeth started her chores that morning, she felt very uneasy. Her first job was to polish all the picture frames in the Great Grand Hall, but when she got there it was already full of people. She spotted Professor Bombast instructing workmen to move bits of expensive scenery into the school theatre.

Of course, thought Elspeth, *they're making the place look good for the Look at Us! show.*

The Look at Us! show was an extra-big and extra-fancy school show. Journalists and lots of Very Important People would come to watch. Professor Bombast barked instructions as two men carefully hung his new portrait over the mantelpiece.

Elspeth looked at the portrait and tried not to laugh. It showed Professor Bombast in a safari suit, baring his teeth and karate-chopping a giant tiger. But Elspeth knew that he had never fought a tiger. Despite all his wild stories, Professor Bombast had never hurt an animal in his life. Elspeth knew for a fact that the tiger-skin rug in the Great Grand Hall was fake, and had been bought from a shop in Hull.

She had overheard Professor Bombast having a whispery phone conversation about it months ago.

As you know, dear reader, when adults are having whispery phone conversations it generally means they are up to no good.

Once Elspeth had finished polishing all the picture frames using a pair of Miss Crabb's old bloomers and some rancid polish, she had to go straight to the kitchens to help with lunch.

"I just need five minutes," she muttered to herself. "Just five minutes to think!"

But there was no chance of that. In the kitchen, Gladys Goulash was plucking hairs from her chin with tweezers, then flicking the hairs into a pot of soup. Miss Crabb was leaning on the kitchen table having her morning snooze.

Gladys Goulash and Miss Crabb were alike in many ways. They were both lazy and greedy, and they both thought children were horrible. The only difference was that Gladys Goulash was very stupid, and Miss Crabb was only stupid some of the time.

Right now, Miss Crabb was twitching and lurching in her sleep, and it looked as though she was going to fall right off her chair and on to the boxes of vegetables lined up beside it.

She caught herself just in time, waking up with an almighty snort and shouting at the first person she saw.

"Hurry up and finish scrubbing those dishes, idiot girl!" Miss Crabb yelled at Elspeth.

"I did them yesterday, Miss Crabb," said Elspeth. "All the dishes are ready for lunch."

"Pah!" Miss Crabb threw a mouldy courgette at Elspeth.

Luckily Elspeth ducked, so it hit Gladys Goulash on the nose and made her drop her tweezers into the pot of soup. Gladys Goulash peered into the pot and shrugged.

"Not those dishes, girl," continued Miss Crabb. "*My* dishes! The ones from my midnight feast two months ago. I found them under my bed this morning."

Elspeth turned round. Stacked up next

to the sink was the most
disgusting pile of dishes she
had ever seen. Mouldy
cheese grew on the side
of the plates. A rat was
nibbling some sticky
black leftovers oozing
down the side of a bowl.

Elspeth sighed and
set about washing Miss
Crabb's disgusting
midnight-feast dishes.
While she worked, she hummed the strange
tune, to see if she could remember any
more words. "Two is for butter, three is for
syrup…" Elspeth sang to herself softly.

She tried to remember the next line, but
it was stuck somewhere in the back of her
mind. So she kept humming quietly all the

way through washing the dishes, and kept on humming while she chopped seventy, eighty, ninety, one hundred manky and oozy courgettes.

As she finished the last courgette, Elspeth had a horrible sensation of being watched. She turned her head slightly to find Miss Crabb standing right behind her, breathing down the back of her neck with an awful scent of tuna fish.

"Interesting little tune," Miss Crabb said, leaning closer. She jabbed Elspeth hard in the ribs. "What's that you're singing?"

Elspeth froze. Miss Crabb was always watching her in a strange way. Sometimes she jumped out from behind doors to frighten Elspeth, as if she wanted to shock her into saying something.

"I don't know, Miss Crabb," Elspeth said.

"It's just a bit of an old song that's stuck in my head."

"Hmmm." Miss Crabb moved away slowly, still staring at her. "Well it is *lovely* to hear a young child singing." She showed her teeth in a horrible grimace that was meant to be a smile. "Do feel free to share your … musical talents … whenever you like." With that Miss Crabb scuttled off across the kitchen, grabbed an old pencil and started scribbling something in a notebook.

Elspeth stared at her. Miss Crabb had never said anything nice to her in the whole year she'd been at the school. "Nice" comments from Miss Crabb gave Elspeth the shivers. And suddenly the dream she had that morning flashed back into her head. The supermarket … her parents …

and Miss Crabb. Elspeth washed up the knife and chopping board as fast as she could, so she could escape from the smelly kitchen. This wasn't just mysterious. This was HIGHLY suspicious.

9
Highly Suspicious Things

That afternoon, Elspeth managed to sneak away while Miss Crabb was fixing her spy camera. The spy camera was a tiny device Miss Crabb had used to spy on a handsome teacher called Mr D'Angelo last term. Mr D'Angelo had been so frightened by Miss Crabb that he left the school in a rush one day and never came back. Elspeth reckoned this was the perfect chance to do some detective work. She was determined to find something – anything – to jog her memory.

Elspeth walked along the corridor of the first floor, pushed open the creaky door to the library and stepped inside. It was completely quiet. None of the show-offs liked reading, so Elspeth knew none of them would be in there.

Professor Bombast used the library as an office because he thought the books made him look extra-clever and important. Elspeth saw that he wasn't in there, either. She sighed in relief.

The library smelled like old leather, polish and books. Hundreds and hundreds of books. Elspeth loved books. They could take her far away from the Pandora Pants School for Show-offs, even if she had to hide behind the curtains and read them very,

very fast. She had read about abandoned children and orphans being rescued by mysterious strangers, and she secretly hoped that one day a rich uncle or aunt might turn up and take her away to live with them. Or even a poor uncle or aunt. So long as they were kind people who didn't make her sleep in a wardrobe and wash mouldy pots.

Elspeth searched through the messy piles of papers and files on Professor Bombast's desk, but everything was such a mess that she couldn't work out where to start. She grabbed a stack of papers and went over to her favourite seat in the window. She started by leafing through a large register, but of course her name was nowhere to be found.

There must be some information about me somewhere, she thought.

Elspeth was just rifling through a big address book when the library door flew open and Professor Bombast marched in and picked up the huge phone on his desk, dialling a number in a very snappy way. He didn't notice Elspeth tucked up on the window seat.

"HELLO!" he bellowed into the receiver. "LOOK, I'VE BEEN EXPECTING THAT STUFFED BEAR FOR THREE WEEKS. WHERE IS IT?"

Very slowly, Elspeth slithered behind one of the big velvet curtains so she wouldn't be seen. It was very dusty so she held her breath and tried not to cough. But unfortunately one of her purple trainers was peeking out.

Professor Bombast slammed down the phone as soon as he saw it.

"WHY, YOU SNEAKY LITTLE POT WASHER! HOW DARE YOU!" he hollered.

Professor Bombast was not a cruel man, but he was not about to let Elspeth Hart get away with listening to his top-secret-

stuffed-animal-buying conversations.

"I'm sorry, Professor Bombast!" stammered Elspeth. "I only came in here to read a book while Miss Crabb was … busy. I didn't know you would come in."

Professor Bombast stared at her for a second, scratching his shock of black hair. His face was slightly purple, which meant he was still angry, but his eyes weren't bulging any more, which meant he was calming down.

"RIGHT! There's only one thing for it," he shouted. "Detention!"

"But Professor Bombast…" Elspeth hesitated for a second, then decided she had nothing to lose. "I don't go to lessons here. How can I be put in detention if I'm not technically one of your pupils?"

As you know, dear reader, Elspeth Hart

was small and shy and wearing a pair of dirty old trainers with scribbles all over them, but she was still the smartest person in the school.

Professor Bombast looked confused.

"Er … quite," he said. "Well, you can tidy up my desk and file every bit of paper on it in alphabetical order!"

Elspeth looked at the desk, piled high with bits of old parchment, receipts, delivery notes from online shops and sweet wrappers.

"Where would I file this?" she asked, holding up a crumpled Chump wrapper.

"Under C, obviously!" shouted Professor Bombast, who was clearly losing his patience again. "You can stay here all afternoon. I shall lock you in, and you'll only get supper if you've finished it by

the time I come back. Oh, and Elspeth –"
Professor Bombast looked very serious –
"these are confidential papers. No need to,
ahem, tell anyone about what you may see."

With that, he marched out.

Elspeth groaned. Professor Bombast's
desk was a mess most of the time and today
it was even worse than usual. But now, at
least, she had the perfect excuse to do a
bit of snooping. She pulled up a chair and
started sorting things into piles.

Elspeth filed all Professor Bombast's
online shopping receipts in one section.

"Don't worry, Professor Bombast, I
won't tell anyone you bought all these
stuffed animals on the internet," she
muttered to herself.

She read Madame Chi-chi's CV, which
showed she had been born in Enfield, not

Italy at all. Elspeth laughed until she almost fell off her chair when she found a picture of Madame Chi-chi. *How funny!* Elspeth thought. *Why on earth would Professor Bombast keep a photo of Madame Chi-chi?*

But there was no sign that Elspeth Hart even existed. No papers or pictures or records at all.

What happened to me on the night of the flood? Elspeth asked herself. She closed her eyes and concentrated as hard as she could. But it was no use. She couldn't remember a thing between going to bed that night and waking up at the Pandora Pants School for Show-offs. Elspeth frowned and began searching through the drawers of Professor Bombast's desk. And just as she was about to give up, she found a dusty, musty old file tied up with red ribbon. And what did it say on the front?

79

10

Well, What Do You Think It Said on the Front?

You are correct! It said on the front, in black inky letters:

If you found a bundle of dusty old papers with your name on the front, dear reader, you might read them immediately. They could contain secrets or stories about you, or your worst school report or embarrassing photos of you on the potty.

But Elspeth Hart was more patient than that. She stared at the bundle for a long while, turning it over in her hands. She was desperate to know what was in the papers, but she also knew that Professor Bombast could be back at any minute.

Quickly and quietly, Elspeth untied the ribbon and slipped the papers from the file on to her lap. Then she stuffed a selection of Professor Bombast's old receipts inside the file and retied the ribbon.

If it's this dusty, nobody's looked at it for months, she told herself. *So no one will notice if the papers inside go missing for a little while.* She stuffed the papers in the waistband of her leggings and waited for Professor Bombast to come back.

Elspeth spent some of the time sneakily trying to guess the password for Professor Bombast's laptop. She tried this most Saturdays when Professor Bombast was having his weekly hair treatment, in the desperate hope that she could email someone to ask for help, but Elspeth never managed to crack the password.

When Professor Bombast did finally unlock the door, he was holding a model horse's head under his arm.

"Perfect for the school show, eh?" he said. "Off you trot, then. And no more spying!"

Professor Bombast took a Chump from his drawer and started munching loudly.

Elspeth raced back up to the attic, expecting Miss Crabb to be angry that she'd been gone so long. But when she got up there, she heard loud cackling.

Elspeth breathed a sigh of relief. It sounded like Miss Crabb and Gladys Goulash were having one of their poker evenings. Miss Crabb was not the sort of person who needed friends, dear reader, but she did like having someone to show off to and boss about. She had been showing off to Gladys Goulash and bossing her about for years. In fact, it was the only reason she kept her around.

Elspeth listened at the door. Gladys Goulash was telling a long story about how a sailor on a cruise had fallen for her and had jumped overboard when she refused to marry him.

Elspeth didn't believe a word of it. Gladys Goulash was shaped like a potato and had a moustache. Elspeth had seen a picture of her as a young woman, and even then she had been shaped like a potato and had a moustache.

"I'm going for a bath now, Miss Crabb," Elspeth said, sticking her head into the room.

Miss Crabb flicked a hand at her, not bothering to turn around. "Don't use the hot water, you little varmint!" she cackled.

Elspeth locked the bathroom door. Her heart was hammering. She ran the taps on full power and took the papers out from her waistband. With shaking hands, she started going through them. There were some forms signed by Professor Bombast, giving the date that Elspeth had arrived at the school. And then there was a letter.

11
And It Wasn't Just Any Old Letter

Dear Professor Bombast,

My niece will be coming to stay with us when I return from my holiday in Skipping Hopton. She is ~~a little varmint~~ good child and will be very useful with the pot washing. Tragically her parents died in a flood two weeks ago and she must never ever be allowed into the school grounds as she is allergic to the fresh air.

Yours,
Miss Crabb

Elspeth stared at the letter, her mind racing. The water kept pouring into the bath, until it was almost overflowing, but Elspeth didn't notice.

Hang on a minute! Elspeth thought. *This letter says my parents were washed away two weeks ago. Not the day before I arrived here, like Miss Crabb told me. She's been lying to me!*

Elspeth wondered why Miss Crabb would lie to her about when the flood happened. And then it dawned on her – maybe there never was a flood. Perhaps her parents were alive after all!

And if the stuff about the flood is a lie, what else is? she wondered. Elspeth's eyes widened. "Allergic to fresh air" had always sounded like the stupidest thing ever, but now she came to think of it, she could remember being in a big garden, jumping up and down on a bouncy castle. *Outside!* she thought. *I'm sure I remember being outside!*

Elspeth thought about that last night at home until her brain started to hurt. The memories weren't clear at all, but it hadn't seemed like the weather for a flood. It hadn't even been raining. She had simply gone to bed as normal and when she woke up, she was in the Pandora Pants School for Show-offs.

Miss Crabb had always been very vague about how Elspeth got to the school. Now, Elspeth was convinced that she was up to no good.

The next day, when Elspeth got to the kitchen to help with lunch, she found Miss

Crabb and Gladys Goulash stirring a massive pot and whispering to each other. They were being unusually secretive, and the fact that Gladys wasn't plucking her chin hairs over the pot was very suspicious. Elspeth kept as quiet as she could and listened very carefully.

"I'm sick of this," Miss Crabb was muttering. "I've tried all the stupid stinking recipes I can find. But it's no good. I need that Extra-special Sticky Toffee Sauce recipe BEFORE THE SCHOOL SHOW!"

"S'pose we could chuck a few more rats' tails in it," wheezed Gladys, giving the mixture a prod with one of her filthy fingers.

Miss Crabb drew herself up to her full height and glared at Gladys with a look that would have shrivelled a stoat.

"When," she demanded in an icy voice,

"when did you put rats' tails in my toffee sauce?"

Gladys shrugged. "Thought it might bulk it up a bit," she said. "Seems to work with all the other meals we cook."

Miss Crabb flared her nostrils, then picked up a sieve full of sludgy spinach and dumped it over Gladys Goulash's head.

"This is NOT JUST ANY RECIPE!" she hissed. "I'm trying to make an extra-special sticky toffee sauce that's as good as Elspeth Hart's secret family recipe."

Miss Crabb took a deep breath. "That little creep knows the ingredients, but she's just too stupid to remember them. If only I'd known how much trouble it would cause to whack her over the head with a baking tray when I was stealing her. It seems to have affected her teeny-tiny brain. But she will remember… I heard her humming something very interesting the other day. And when I get my hands on that recipe, I am going to take over the world!"

Gladys scratched her head. A few flakes of dandruff and some bits of spinach fell into the toffee sauce.

"How are you going to take over the world with toffee sauce?" she asked.

"Because this is a recipe that Elspeth's drippy parents were working on for ages," said Miss Crabb crossly. "It's supposed to be the most delicious toffee sauce in the ENTIRE WORLD. Once we've figured out how to make it, everyone will want some and we'll be millionaires! I spotted Elspeth's parents when I was on holiday at the coast last year. Every night I'd nick my dinner from the CheapAsChips supermarket, and they were always popping in to buy more and more sugar. 'Dodgy,' I told myself. 'These folk are up to something.' So I followed them home one day and saw what they were doing."

"Ooh," Gladys Goulash said. "What was they up to?"

"Making an extra-special sticky toffee sauce, you idiot!" Miss Crabb said. "Why do you think I stole Elspeth? I heard them saying they'd finally cracked the recipe, and it would be safe with Elspeth. She's got that recipe in her head, I'm sure of it!"

Gladys Goulash prodded at the sauce with a sausagey finger and snorted. "Wot was you doing shoplifting in CheapAsChips?"

"You greasy gibbon," Miss Crabb hissed. "The wages here ain't exactly generous, are they?" Miss Crabb gazed into the distance and a creepy smile appeared on her face. "I've been short of cash for a long time, Gladys Goulash. Remember after I got out of prison? I was a lollipop lady and a fake dentist, but I kept getting the sack. I ain't cut out for the working life. We'll be millionaires once I get that recipe, though! We can sell this stuff to Horrads, the fancy department store! I've got a boyfriend who knows people there."

"Boyfriend?" Gladys looked confused.

"He's called Ivan Firensky," Miss Crabb

replied, "and he's ever so handsome. He's going to help me sell the sauce. We'll never have to wash another pot again, Gladys Goulash!" Miss Crabb wiped a streak of sauce from her chin. "He's in a hurry, though. Says we need the recipe in time for the Look at Us! show. He's got a plan."

Elspeth felt sick. *Miss Crabb isn't my aunt,* she thought. *She STOLE me! And Tatiana's dad is mixed up in all this, too...* Elspeth carefully snuck back out of the door and hurried down the corridor to find Rory. As she walked, the song appeared again, running through her head... "Four is for vanilla ... five is for treacle..." Elspeth paused and let the tune take over.

It couldn't be... she thought. *Could it? And then, in a flash, it came to her. Yes! I know what that strange song means!*

93

12
That Strange Song

Elspeth grabbed Rory's arm as soon as he came out of the classroom, pulling him into an alcove on the stairs.

"Elspeth! What's going on?" Rory asked. He looked around to see if anyone had spotted them.

"I found out something big," Elspeth said quickly, before she could lose Rory's attention. He always worried that the other show-offs might see him talking to Elspeth, and make his life even more miserable.

"I mean really BIG!" she hurried on. She filled him in on the letter she'd found in the library, and the conversation she'd just heard. "Miss Crabb isn't my aunt after all!" she said breathlessly. "She stole me because she thinks I have a secret recipe that can make her rich. And I think the weird tune I've had stuck in my head contains the ingredients for that recipe. Rory, I need your help. I know Tatiana's got it in for me – but it turns out Miss Crabb is even more dangerous than her!"

Rory paused, trying to take it all in. "Elspeth," he said, "what are you going on about? How could a song have ingredients for a recipe?"

"Oh, it's simple!" Elspeth couldn't get the words out fast enough. She sang the first few lines. *"One is for sugar, two is for butter...* Do you see? I can't remember the whole recipe – but those HAVE to be the ingredients!"

"OK, OK." Rory nodded. Then he frowned. "But if Miss Crabb isn't your aunt, how would she know about the recipe?"

"She was spying on us!" said Elspeth. She paused, thinking how to explain everything to Rory without sounding crazy. "The other night I had this dream that I was with Mum and Dad, and Miss Crabb was spying on us. In a supermarket. But it must have actually happened... I heard Miss Crabb tell Gladys Goulash she was spying on my parents, trying to get their recipe! I think everything Miss Crabb has told me is a lie.

I bet I'm not even allergic to fresh air!"

Rory was looking troubled. "Spying on you? In a *supermarket*? Are you sure you've got this right? I mean, if we go accusing Miss Crabb of stuff like that, we could end up in real trouble."

"Don't be such a baby!" Elspeth said without thinking. Then she caught sight of her friend's worried face and felt awful. "Sorry. I know it's scary. But I need your help, Rory. I can't trust anyone else!"

"I'll think about it, I promise," Rory said, hurrying away to his next class. "Sorry, Elspeth, I've got to run. Speak to you later."

Elspeth watched him go, feeling lost. Rory had never rushed away from her like that before. She looked down at her shoes for a minute, feeling sad. But the doodles on her trainers reminded her of her dad and she knew she had to be brave. She decided to head to the library again. She could return the papers and figure out what to do next.

The library was locked, but Professor Bombast had left the key in the door. Elspeth took the key and locked the door from the inside. If anyone came along, they'd think it was Professor Bombast inside. And if Professor Bombast came along, he'd probably get confused and go searching for the key.

As Elspeth hurried over to the desk, something caught her eye. Sitting on top was a shoebox with a bright red ribbon tied around it and a silver rosette on top. And it had her name on it.

Elspeth narrowed her eyes. *That's weird,* she thought. *Nobody in the school would ever buy me a present … would they?* She stepped closer to the box. There was a small gift tag on it. Gently, Elspeth lifted it up. It said:

A gift for Elspeth Hart, who works so hard in our exsellent school.

Elspeth was good at spelling. She knew loads of words from all the books she had hidden in the library and read. Excellent was spelled with a "c", not an "s", she was sure. Who had written the tag?

Obviously not Professor Bombast. Professor Bombast was weird, but he was quite good at spelling. It wasn't Madame Chi-chi's handwriting, which was swirly and huge and usually in glittery pen. It wasn't Madame Stringy, either, who preferred to "communicate through the beauty of music", which meant she was rubbish at reading and writing. And there was no way that Miss Crabb or Gladys Goulash would ever buy a present for Elspeth – especially not a present that looked exactly like a brand-new pair of trainers in her size.

Cautiously, Elspeth leaned towards the box and sniffed it. Instantly, the pong of Tatiana Firensky's perfume hit her. It was an exclusive fragrance created by the fashion designer Jean-Paul Goatherd, which smelled like a very posh old lady who had fallen into a vat of vanilla pudding. Elspeth would have known that smell anywhere.

She understood then that the present was an evil trick. As she lifted up the box, she heard a scrabbling sound. The sound of something alive.

13
The Scrabbling Sound
in the Shoebox

Very, very slowly, Elspeth set the box down
where she had found it. She didn't scream
or run away. She just took a little step
backwards, and then another little step
backwards. She wiggled her toes in her too-
tight trainers, which is what she did when
she was thinking about things, and then she
placed her hands behind her back and had

another think about things.

It could be a box full of spiders. The scrabbling sound wasn't loud enough for it to be one of the giant rats that roamed the halls. What else could it be? Cockroaches?

There were plenty of cockroaches running around the kitchen, but Professor Bombast made sure they weren't seen in the school. Every so often, Gladys Goulash would sweep up the dead ones, fry them up in honey, and serve them as a special desert in the canteen with a splodge of cream. Elspeth decided to find out what was in the box.

If, dear reader, you are ever offered a present that looks like a pair of your favourite trainers, but makes a sound as though it might be a box of insects, it is better to check before running away

ungratefully. Always
remember that.

Elspeth untied the
ribbon around the
shoebox. She put the card
to one side. And gently, very gently, she
lifted the lid up a tiny bit and peeked in.

What she saw made her slam the lid back
down. It was Lazlo. And he was angry.

Elspeth knew that anyone taking the lid
off a box where Lazlo had been trapped was
likely to be bitten on the nose immediately.
She sighed. Cockroaches were one thing,
but this was something else.

"Tatiana Firensky," she said as she tied
up the box extra tightly, "this time, you have
gone too far."

As the huge grandfather clock in the Great Grand Hall struck seven, Elspeth sat down at the very top of the staircase. She placed the shoebox containing Lazlo beside her. She knew Rory would be beside himself with worry while Lazlo was gone, but she needed a minute to think before she found him.

She made an important list in her head. It had five points:

1) Miss Crabb is NOT my aunt. She stole me from my parents. If she's lying about that, maybe the flood never even happened!
2) Miss Crabb thinks I have my parents' Extra-special Sticky Toffee Sauce recipe.
3) The song is definitely the ingredients for a recipe ... I just can't remember the rest of it.

4) I bet I'm not allergic to fresh air, so I can escape!

5) Tatiana Firensky has a face like a pig stuck in a gate.

The last point on the list wasn't strictly necessary, but it made Elspeth laugh when she thought about it, which was a good enough reason for adding it.

I just have to find a way to escape from Miss Crabb and her evil plans, Elspeth thought. *And if I could get Tatiana Firensky to shut up at the same time, that would be perfect!*

14
Elspeth Hart's Secret Recipe

Elspeth Hart was looking for Rory. To find him, all she had to do was walk up and down the stairs, listening for the sound of wailing. Rory hated to be without Lazlo.

Elspeth paused outside Madame Stringy's music rooms. Sure enough, the crying was so loud that it echoed through the soundproof walls.

Pushing open the door, all Elspeth could
see was a huge pile of balled-up tissues.
Then she spotted Rory Snitter lying on
his stomach and pounding his fists on
the floor. He had definitely taken Lazlo's
disappearance hard.

"Laaaaaazlo!" wailed Rory Snitter. "My
Laaaaazlo! Wherefore art thou Lazlo?"

Rory had cried so much that there was
a small river of tears running down the
middle of the room.

Elspeth sighed. Rory was her
friend, but he was acting like
the worst of the show-offs.
She wished he was a bit
braver. That way he
could help her escape.

"Rory? I've got something for you,"
Elspeth said. She closed the door behind
her and kneeled down next to him. "Look!
Don't cry. It's Lazlo. He's fine!"

Instantly, Rory sat up. "Lazlo?" he asked.
He wiped his nose on his sleeve. "You found
Lazlo?"

He grabbed the box and hauled Lazlo
out, kissing him on the head. Lazlo bit him
on the nose. No matter how much you love a
pet, dear reader, always remember that they
have not been brought up to have manners.
Sometimes they do the nastiest things when
you are only trying to help them.

Rory ignored the drips of blood that
were gathering on his snotty nose. A smile
crept over his damp face.

"LAZLO! You're back!" he cried. He
looked at Elspeth. "Where was he? I was so

worried. You didn't take him for a joke, did you?"

"No way! You know I wouldn't do that," Elspeth said indignantly. "I found him in the library. He was in this shoebox. I think Tatiana stole him so she could play a trick on me. You know he always attacks when he's been cooped up."

As if to prove her point, Lazlo bit Rory again on the ear and then peed all over his shoulder.

"You know what Tatiana is like," Elspeth carried on. "We all do."

"Yes," Rory said. "And sticking Lazlo in a shoebox sounds like the kind of thing she'd do, too. But if any of us said anything, her parents would file an Official Filthy Rich Complaint and then we'd never be seen again. They can make people vanish, Elspeth."

Elspeth nodded. "She's really got it in for me. And now I know what Miss Crabb is up to, I have to get out of here."

"Maybe you can escape and go straight to the police," Rory said. "They'll help you, Elspeth!"

Elspeth frowned. "No," she said. "I don't want to do that. I can't be sure that my parents are still alive. If they're not…" She swallowed. "You know what will happen – they'll send me to live with another family, or I'll have to stay in a children's home or something."

"That wouldn't be so bad. They might be nice," Rory said.

"NO!" Elspeth's voice came out louder than she meant it to. "I've spent a whole year locked up in this place with other children and stupid rules and I just want to be back in my OWN HOME." Elspeth realized she was crying. She wiped her eyes, feeling embarrassed.

Rory looked at Lazlo for a second. Then he looked up at Elspeth, reached out and gave her an awkward pat on the shoulder. "I want to help you," he said. "I was being a baby about it before. But we need to stick together. I'll do whatever I can to help you get out of here."

Elspeth blew her nose on the clean tissue Rory was offering her, then smiled at him. "That is the best news I've had for a long time," she said. "And I think I've got the start of a plan."

Meanwhile, Tatiana Firensky was on the phone to her father. She had a special pink phone covered in glittery diamonds, which was so heavy that she had to get someone else to hold it for her while she had a conversation. At the moment, Octavia Ornamento was struggling to keep it up with both hands.

"Oh, do shut up, Daddy, none of that was my fault," whined Tatiana, filing her nails with a pink emery board. She prodded Octavia Ornamento with the nail file to make her lift the phone higher. Octavia's puny arms were trembling with the effort. Octavia could just make out the voice on the other end of the phone. Tatiana's father sounded absolutely furious.

"I didn't let the racehorses out of the paddock last time I was home," she said. "Somebody obviously stole them. Why would I take your prize-winning horses?"

Tatiana's mouth twitched as she said this. She had paid one of her father's gardeners to steal three racehorses and sell them on the black market. Tatiana had taken most of the profit and used it to buy a very expensive gold-plated mirror and ten pairs of Jean-Paul Goatherd designer shoes.

On the other end of the phone, Ivan Firensky had moved on to a new subject.

"Yes, of course I'll be the star of the Look at Us! show," Tatiana hissed into the phone, rolling her eyes. "I'm so much prettier and more talented than all the idiots here. And I hope you'll make sure Professor Bombast knows I'm the star of the show. You will, won't you, Daddy?" Tatiana paused, listening, and then raised her eyebrows. "Plan? What plan, Daddy?"

Just then, Octavia keeled over and

collapsed on the floor, crying quietly and massaging her arms. Tatiana picked up the phone and stepped daintily over her weeping friend, ignoring her completely. She wandered into the next room, still talking on the phone. "Outer Mongolia? But what about me, Daddy?"

Ivan Firensky gave a long reply that made a smug smile spread right over Tatiana's face.

"Extra-special Sticky Toffee Sauce! How super! It's a terribly clever idea, Daddy. Don't worry, I shan't breathe a word to anyone. No, not even Mummy."

Tatiana ended the call with a satisfied smile. She liked nothing better than a secret plan.

15

Ivan Firensky's Top-secret Plan

Professor Bombast was feeling very worried. He was quite sure the stress of his job was making his hair fall out. He had just dealt with a furious phone call from a mother because her child had been sent home with food poisoning – the third child to get food poisoning at the school in the last week. Professor Bombast was starting to wonder if Miss Crabb was doing a good enough job in the kitchens.

"Oh dear, oh dear," he muttered. He munched two Chump bars in a row and tried to think of a solution. He was losing pupils fast, and the west wing of the school was definitely falling down – Madame Stringy had taken a nasty tumble last night on the rotting stairs. He needed money, and he needed it at once. Professor Bombast groaned as he remembered the expensive stuffed bear he'd bought for the library. He wished he'd never bought it, but he couldn't help himself. Collecting stuffed animals was his favourite thing ever!

Just then, the phone rang. "Pandora Pants School for Show-offs," Professor Bombast droned into the receiver while staring angrily at all the stuffed animals he'd spent his money on.

"Bombast, you old fruit, I've decided to make a generous donation to the school," bellowed the voice on the other end. "A VERY GENEROUS DONATION."

Professor Bombast knew the voice at once. It was Ivan Firensky. Of all the pushy, bossy parents he had to deal with, Ivan Firensky was the pushiest and bossiest. But his daughter Tatiana was clearly going to be famous, and that would be good for the school's reputation. So Professor Bombast had to put up with both of them.

"That's, um, very kind of you, Mr Firensky," Professor Bombast said. "How … er … how much exactly?"

"TWO MILLION POUNDS!" Ivan Firensky's voice boomed down the phone. "On one condition. That my darling

daughter is the ONLY star of your Look
at Us! show. She must be the centre of
attention! Do you understand me, old fruit?"

Two hours later, Professor Bombast was
teaching the Attention Seeking in General
class and wondering what he'd let himself in
for. He had agreed to take Ivan Firensky's
money and make Tatiana the star, but
looking at Tatiana's sour face, he realized
this might have been a terrible mistake.

The class were forming a huge human
pyramid, and Tatiana was supposed to be
at the top. Working with other pupils was
not her strong point, however. She was
kicking the other children underneath her,
and complaining loudly that her hair was
getting messed up.

"Teamwork, chaps, teamwork!" Professor Bombast called, trying to sound jolly.

"Rah! I don't think so!" Tatiana gave a vicious wriggle and leaped down.

With a lot of screams and shouts, the pyramid of show-offs came tumbling to the ground. Half the class, naturally, burst into tears on the spot. If you have ever taken a tumble in gym class, dear reader, you will know that those soft blue mats are actually quite painful to land on.

Professor Bombast rubbed his forehead. "Class dismissed," he said weakly.

Elspeth Hart was watching at the side of the room. A clever plan was starting to form in her mind. The Look at Us! show was going to be VERY interesting this year.

16
The Night Before the Very Important Look at Us! Show

Elspeth was feeling excited about her big escape. In fact, she was trying not to smirk to herself as she climbed the stairs towards the attic that evening. That was, until she saw Miss Crabb looming above her, with a horrible fake smile fixed on her face.

"Elspeth, dear," Miss Crabb crooned, "I do believe you have a little recipe, and I do believe it's meant for me."

Elspeth stared back at her angrily. "I don't know what you're talking about, Miss Crabb," she said. "I don't have any recipe. I never did." She wanted to shout, "Tell me the truth about my parents, you old bat!" but she stopped herself, just in case Miss Crabb locked her in the cellar.

"Oh, I think you do," Miss Crabb said. She came down one step and jutted her pointy chin towards Elspeth. Elspeth could smell her disgusting breath. "I think you have a special recipe, and you've been hiding it from me, and it's time you gave it to me."

Elspeth stood her ground. "I don't have anything," she said. "Nothing. I came here in just my clothes and shoes. You know that."

Miss Crabb was starting to shake with rage. "Oh, I don't think it's written down," she said icily. "I think you've memorized it." She reached out a clawed hand and grabbed Elspeth's arm. "If you don't give me that recipe, I am going to offer Tatiana Firensky's father the chance to have you as Tatiana's free Personal Assistant. Which means you will have to be with her at all times, run around after her, brush her hair for her, and do ANYTHING SHE SAYS."

Elspeth gulped. This was by far the worst punishment Miss Crabb had ever come up with – much much worse than being locked in the cellar or forced to trim gnarly toenails. She knew Tatiana would jump at the chance of having a Personal Assistant.

Elspeth wriggled out of Miss Crabb's grasp and sprinted back down the stairs. She bumped into Rory and Lazlo just as they were wandering across the Great Grand Hall.

"Come with me!" Elspeth hissed. They ran into the theatre and clambered into their secret hiding place under the stage.

Lazlo kept a watchful eye out for rats and mice. Elspeth told Rory about Miss Crabb's latest threat.

"Being Tatiana's Personal Assistant

would be the worst thing ever," Elspeth said in exasperation. "Nobody stands up to her, that's the problem. Not even the teachers! But I've got a plan, Rory. I'm only spending one more night in this awful place. I'm going to escape."

"Well," Rory said bravely, "I want to come with you."

"Really?" Elspeth hadn't expected this. "Are you sure?"

"Of course I am!" Rory sounded very confident all of a sudden. "Elspeth, I hate it here. I'm not as loud as the other children, I don't even care about being famous, and Lazlo is very upset after being stuck in that box. He's off his food and everything."

"OK," said Elspeth, thinking fast. "We'll get you out of here as well." She took a deep breath, trying to steady her nerves. "Tomorrow is the big day. When Tatiana's doing her routine in the Look at Us! show, everyone will be distracted. We'll sneak out of school and jump in the first limo we see. All the parents will have their chauffeur-driven cars waiting outside. We'll get the driver to take us to a train station. If they don't want to cooperate—"

"They won't," interrupted Rory.

"Then we will just have to get Lazlo to bite them. Nobody wants to mess with a bad-tempered lizard. They'll be so freaked out that they will do whatever we need them to."

Rory was looking even more worried than usual. "Elspeth, you know I want to escape with you, but this plan is really dangerous," he whispered. "And what if you really are allergic to fresh air?"

"Don't worry!" Elspeth said confidently. "Miss Crabb was lying the whole time... I'm not allergic to fresh air at all."

Elspeth tried to feel as brave as she sounded. This was her only chance. She had to be ready.

17
And Are You Ready, Dear Reader?

It was the morning of the day of the very important Look at Us! show. Nobody had slept very well the night before.

Professor Bombast had cuddled Cutie-pie for half an hour, unable to sleep. Eventually he had marched around the Great Grand Hall in his tartan pyjamas, making sure his new portrait was perfectly straight on the wall.

Tatiana Firensky had dreadful nightmares about which designer shoes to wear for the performance.

Octavia Ornamento had horrible dreams about being forced to hold an incredibly heavy phone for hours at a time until her arms stopped working.

Esmerelda Higginsbot dreamed of pushing Tatiana Firensky face first into a muddy puddle, then woke up suddenly, wondering if Tatiana could read her mind.

Miss Crabb dreamed about losing her false teeth.

Gladys Goulash had nightmares about having to wash, as she was planning her annual bath for the next day.

Elspeth Hart couldn't sleep, either. She was nervous and excited and scared and hopeful all at the same time. The words of the song kept drifting through her head, and whenever she started to drop off, she had visions of huge vats of sticky toffee sauce, which woke her up with a jolt. She was just falling asleep as the sun came up, but then she was woken by an awful screeching sound coming from the dormitories.

"MY HAIR! My beautiful perfect hair! AAAAARGH!"

It sounded like Esmerelda Higginsbot.

Elspeth crept out of bed and down the stairs to the girls' dormitories. There was a massive crowd outside the room Esmerelda shared with Tatiana, and everyone was whispering and staring. Elspeth paused on the staircase and craned her neck so she could see into the room.

Esmerelda was sitting at her dressing table, weeping. Every so often she would glance up, look in the mirror and scream "MY HAIR!" all over again.

Someone had chopped off all Esmerelda's beautiful long dark hair in the night. Her hair was now a tufty mess that looked a bit like the old brush Miss Crabb gave Elspeth to use when she was washing the pots.

"Oh dear, dear, dear," Tatiana simpered. She was perched on Esmerelda's bed trying to look sympathetic. "What a frightful disaster. Who on earth would do this to you?" She glanced round at the watching crowd. "Who was it?" she asked sharply.

"Hmm?" She eyeballed Elspeth. "Surely none of the PUPILS here would do this?"

All the show-offs turned to Elspeth.

Elspeth stared back at Tatiana. "It wasn't me and you know it," she said calmly.

Tatiana gave a snort. "Well, I'd say you're the PRIME SUSPECT," she muttered, which made Esmerelda start crying even more loudly. "I should think someone will file an Official Filthy Rich Complaint as soon as the show is over."

Elspeth felt ill at the thought of it, but she ignored Tatiana and went quietly back up the stairs. She didn't have to think very hard to know who'd chopped off Esmerelda's hair. "You are not blaming this one on me, Tatiana," Elspeth said to herself, "because I am getting out of here."

18
The Day of the
Look at Us! Show

The Look at Us! show was going to be
terribly impressive, everyone could tell.
The journalists had already written
"terribly impressive" in their notebooks
so they could have a nap during the show
instead of writing their reviews.

Camera crews had arrived to broadcast
the entire performance on live TV, knocking

over several valuable vases in the Great Grand Hall as they came in. Rows and rows of smartly dressed people filled the theatre, and Tatiana Firensky's father had the best seat, right at the front. Professor Bombast had a fixed grin on his face as he welcomed all the pushy parents, who shook his hand with bone-crushing grips.

Then darkness fell. There was a hush. The show was about to begin.

"Ladies and gentlemen," boomed Professor Bombast from behind the curtain. "I present to you ... this year's show-offs!"

The camera crews jostled each other for the best position as the curtain went up. Unfortunately it went up too quickly, and everyone caught a glimpse of Madame Chichi kissing Professor Bombast with a wet smacking sound. It left a big red lipstick mark on his face. But let us not dwell on that disgusting kissing image, dear reader.

The audience shuffled in their seats. The first half of the Look at Us! show would feature performances from all of the show-offs, then the entire second half of the show would be dedicated to Tatiana Firensky. She would be performing a ballet solo from *Swan Lake*, followed by a bit of Shakespeare, followed by a tap dance.

A few people commented that it was odd to have one student take up the second half of the show, but they were quickly hustled out by the massive bodyguards that Tatiana's father had brought in.

Miss Crabb and Gladys Goulash were sniggering in a corner. Miss Crabb stopped sniggering when Ivan Firensky marched towards her. He whispered something in her ear and Rory, who was watching from the side of the hall, sneaked up behind them to listen.

"Well?" Ivan Firensky was saying in a low voice. "Where's the recipe?

"I ain't got it yet!" said Miss Crabb. "It's in her head, but that stupid Elspeth can't seem to remember all the ingredients."

"Get it from her. Get it NOW!" said Ivan Firensky tensely. Then he seemed to remember something and smiled at Miss Crabb sweetly. "We have ways of getting the information," he said. "If you can't get her to remember, I will make sure she does."

"Gah! I'll get it." Miss Crabb glanced from left to right. "Who else knows about our plan?"

"Just us," hissed Ivan Firensky. "And my darling daughter, of course. I had to warn her that today would be VERY special indeed. A school concert that nobody will ever forget!"

"Eee-hee-hee! No more horrible children to cook for!" cackled Miss Crabb.

They both started laughing in an evil way. Neither of them noticed the small nervous face of Rory Snitter, who was hidden behind the bulk of a mean-looking bodyguard, listening to every word.

19
The Time Before
It Was Time for
Tatiana's Performance

Rory ran backstage and grabbed Elspeth, who was tying her shoelaces in double knots in preparation for her escape.

"Elspeth, there's something seriously weird going on. If Miss Crabb doesn't get the recipe from you, Tatiana's father is going to force you to remember all the ingredients!"

"Uh-oh," Elspeth said. "They're a dangerous combination. What else did you hear?"

"Not much. Except Ivan Firensky said Tatiana's the only person who knows about their plan. But whatever they're going to do today, it sounds bad. Let's get out of here."

"OK," Elspeth said. She looked around, flustered. "No, wait."

"What? Elspeth, hurry up! We need to move!" Rory was starting to panic, Elspeth could tell. Lazlo was hopping up and down on his shoulder.

"What did Miss Crabb and Ivan Firensky say exactly?" Elspeth asked.

"Something about … this being a school concert that nobody would forget," Rory said. "And then Miss Crabb said something about not having to deal with horrible children any more."

Elspeth was quiet for a minute.

"What are they plotting? It's me they want – they think I've got the secret recipe. But it sounds like they're up to something else, too." She paused again, thinking hard. "No more horrible children… I think the whole school is in danger. We need to find out what's really going on."

Rory sighed. "We can't find out – Tatiana will never tell you anything. And the show-offs aren't your friends… Can't we just run?"

"No, we can't!" Elspeth said. "I know the show-offs are annoying, but Miss Crabb and Ivan Firensky are pure evil. We need to put a stop to them."

"OK, OK," Rory said. "Tatiana would tell one of her friends, wouldn't she? Octavia's a bit dim – can we get her to help us?"

"Maybe…" Elspeth thought about it. "Yes, that's a good idea. We can send Octavia to talk to Tatiana, and get her to report back to us! But first, wait here. I'm going to run to Miss Crabb's room and get something. Don't move!"

Elspeth raced upstairs. She had to go through piles of old porridge-stained blouses and horrible sweaty vests before she found Miss Crabb's spy camera, wrapped in a dirty cardigan. She ran downstairs with a brilliant idea buzzing round her head.

"What on earth are you up to?" asked Rory, when Elspeth got back.

"The camera is so we can record Tatiana without her knowing about it! It's so small she won't even know she's being taped. We've just got to work out how Octavia can get Tatiana talking about what her father and Miss Crabb are up to. And this is where I need your help, Rory," Elspeth said. "Octavia won't trust me – none of the show-offs do. Can you get her to go and talk to Tatiana?"

Rory thought for a moment, then nodded. "Leave it with me," he said, taking the spy camera from Elspeth.

He hurried down the corridor to the spot where Octavia was practising her tap-dancing routine. "Hello, Octavia, what a nice routine," Rory said. "May I see that wonderful top hat?"

Octavia beamed at him as she handed over the hat, and Rory managed to clip on the little spy camera without her noticing a thing.

"Octavia, I think you might be needed for

a special mission," Rory said.

Octavia looked excited.

"It's Tatiana, you see. She's feeling a bit nervous. You could go and give her a pep talk! You know – tell her she's great, ask her about the classes she's taking next term … that kind of thing."

"OK." Octavia nodded. Then a deep frown creased her pretty forehead. "Tatiana never gets nervous," she said.

"Oh, she is today – it's such a big show!" Rory said, gently steering Octavia towards Tatiana's dressing room. "You'll do a super job of cheering her up."

Octavia wrinkled her nose then trotted off.

Elspeth and Rory waited for a second, then followed her. They pressed their ears to the door and listened carefully.

"Um, hello, Tatiana," Octavia said eventually.

"Oh, it's you," Tatiana replied in a bored voice. "Do up my ballet shoes for me."

There was a long silence.

"Your hair looks nice," Octavia said finally.

"I know," Tatiana said smugly. "It always does."

"So … which classes are you taking next term?" Octavia asked.

Outside the door, Elspeth and Rory exchanged a worried look. Octavia sounded like a robot. Surely even Tatiana Firensky would realize something was up?

"Next term? What are you on about?" said Tatiana. She broke into peals of evil chilling laughter. "I won't be here next term. Ha! But I can't tell you why. It's top secret!"

"Huh?" Octavia said.

"Oh, I might as well tell you," Tatiana said, waving a hand in the air. "You're too pathetic to do anything about it. The secret is … after tonight, this school won't even exist. Daddy is taking over the place!"

Tatiana picked up her mirror and looked at herself as she spoke. "Daddy has sold all the stupid pupils to his friend who has a factory in Outer Mongolia. Then he can use the whole school to make vats of Extra-special Sticky Toffee Sauce with Miss Crabb!" Tatiana stroked her shiny hair. "Let's just say Professor Bombast will be offered a job elsewhere that he can't resist. He'll be signing the papers right now, I should think! Ha!"

"But what will happen to all of us?" Octavia asked.

Tatiana snorted. "I don't care. A private

plane will take you all away this evening. Your parents will think it's a school trip, but no one will be coming back! I should think you will work in the factory and be treated like slaves. But I shall be at a special ballet, tap and showing-off school that is opening in New York. So HA!"

Outside, Elspeth shivered with horror. Ivan Firensky's plot was even worse than she had thought. But the longer Tatiana spoke for, the better Elspeth's plan would turn out.

She listened as Tatiana drivelled on for a bit longer about how stupid all the children and teachers in the school were.

"Of course Elspeth wasn't really rescued from a flood," Tatiana was saying airily. "Daddy told me the whole story yesterday. Miss Crabb kidnapped her. She bashed Elspeth on the head with a baking tray and everything! Isn't that simply hilarious? AND Miss Crabb thinks Daddy is going to marry her!" Tatiana seemed to find this all highly amusing. "But Daddy is just *pretending* to love Miss Crabb so he can use her to get the recipe for the Extra-special

Sticky Toffee Sauce!"

"But Elspeth is an orphan," said Octavia. Her brain wasn't working fast enough to keep up with all Tatiana's news. She was still on the bit about Elspeth. "If Miss Crabb doesn't look after her, who will?"

"I don't care, do I?" Tatiana was saying crossly. "It's about time that stinky little shoe wiper got kicked out."

Elspeth froze.

"Don't get annoyed!" Rory whispered. "We've got exactly what we needed! I'm going in to get the camera right now."

He knocked on the door. "Um, Tatiana? A huge cake has been delivered for you," he called. "A cake with your face on it. But it'll only fit through the door if Octavia leaves."

"Super!" squealed Tatiana. The door flew open and Octavia was shoved out into the hall. Tatiana peered around her. "Where is it?" she asked. "Where's my cake?"

"They're just parking the delivery van," said Elspeth. She grabbed Octavia's hand. "Come on! We'd better go and help them, in case they smudge the icing!"

As soon as they were round the corner, Elspeth unclipped the spy camera from Octavia's top hat. She dug around in her pocket and found the little cable that would connect it to a computer. "Rory," she said calmly, "go and pop this in Professor Bombast's laptop."

20
Professor Bombast's Fancy Laptop

Professor Bombast had programmed his laptop to show films of himself on a large screen between acts. So far the audience had been treated to Professor Bombast winning an Olympic medal, having breakfast with the queen, and arm-wrestling a polar bear. Some of the scenes looked extremely fake, but nobody said anything.

Elspeth and Octavia slipped into the back of the hall. There was a lot of fidgeting going on and one man was eating some very noisy crisps.

But then the large screen on the stage froze. The picture of Professor Bombast doing high-kicks in a karate outfit shuddered and shimmered. And then, very suddenly, the screen went black.

Elspeth held her breath. "Come on, Rory," she prayed. "Please make this work."

Slowly the screen fizzed to life and a grainy picture appeared. Then a loud, annoying voice sounded. It was Tatiana Firensky. And it was obvious that she had been filmed secretly. The audience sat up.

After tonight, this school won't even exist. Daddy is taking over the place!

Elspeth hardly dared to look around

the hall. Everyone's eyes were fixed on the screen. There was total silence, apart from the sound of Tatiana's voice.

A private plane will take you all away this evening. Your parents will think it's a school trip, but no one will be coming back! … Daddy is just pretending *to love Miss Crabb so he can use her to get the recipe for the Extra-special Sticky Toffee Sauce!*

And just as Elspeth squeezed her eyes shut and held her breath, there was a low murmur in the room. It was the sound of a lot of people getting angry. And gradually, it turned into a ROAR.

All the journalists and Very Important People started shouting and demanding answers. The TV presenters leaped up and started to report from right in front of the stage.

Professor Bombast looked furious. He strode towards Ivan Firensky. Ivan Firensky roared for his bodyguards, but nobody came. He decided to make a run for it as a lot of angry parents started hitting him with popcorn and sweets.

"You can't get away with this, Firensky!" shrieked one lady, waving her walking stick.

Meanwhile, Miss Crabb and Gladys Goulash were making a dash for the exit.

I say "making a dash", dear reader, because it sounds quite dramatic, but it was taking them a while.

Miss Crabb shoved her way through the crowds of children, jabbing people with her sharp elbows, but Gladys Goulash slowed her down by clinging on to her skirt.

"Wait for me, you spiky old stick insect!" she yelled.

Gladys Goulash hated moving quickly. She hadn't done any exercise since 2006 when she ran away from the scene of a crime, and she wasn't about to start now.

Unfortunately for Miss Crabb and Gladys Goulash, the disturbance to the show had seriously upset all the show-offs. Most of them had been sniffling quietly

ever since Tatiana had appeared on the
screen. And by the time the news about
the evil plan broke out, there was full-on
blubbering. They were all crying so much
that a shiny pool of snot had appeared in the
middle of the hall. And did Miss Crabb spot
it in time to scoot around it?

No, dear reader, she did not.

She slithered and squealed and slid so
fast across the snot that her legs shot out
from under her and she ended up lying
in it face down. Gladys Goulash flew
through the air and landed on top of her
with a horrible
squelching
sound.

21
The Horrible Squelching
Sound of Snot

Rory stepped forward and prodded them both. "Out for the count," he said wisely. Lazlo leaped down from his shoulder and bit both Miss Crabb and Miss Goulash on the nose. They didn't move.

Elspeth sighed with relief. "Right," she said, "we need to get out of here at once!"

Octavia pulled at her arm. "I think

Tatiana's daddy is leaving now," she whispered.

Sure enough, Ivan Firensky had started scurrying towards the door.

"Catch him, he's not getting away with this!" Elspeth shouted, running after him.

Elspeth was a good runner, and her trainers were ideal for sprinting across the polished hall at high speed, but Rory wasn't so lucky. His dance shoes sent him skidding along with Lazlo clinging on to his shoulder.

As fast as Elspeth ran, she wasn't quick enough. By the time she'd reached the Great Grand Hall, Ivan Firensky was at the main door of the school. As he sprinted, Elspeth could see him taking a pot of Firensky Super-strength Glue out of his jacket pocket. The door slammed shut behind him and there was a sticky squelchy sound.

Elspeth tried to prise the heavy black door open, but it was stuck fast. She shouted out in frustration. Tatiana's dad was going to get away with it! The TV crews were broadcasting live, so the police had to be on their way, but by the time they arrived, Ivan Firensky would be miles away!

"Elspeth, we need to get out of here," Rory muttered.

"I know. If we all pull together, we might be able to unstick the door!" Elspeth said.

"No, no, that's not what I mean," said Rory. Lazlo was jumping up and down on his shoulder, which made Rory look even more worried. "It's Tatiana. Look," he pointed.

Elspeth turned around and gasped in horror. Tatiana Firensky was marching

towards her at high
speed, holding a
pair of diamond-
covered scissors.

"Don't
worry. I'm
sure she's not
viole—" said
Rory, but before
he could finish, there was
a loud whooshing sound and the scissors
flew through the air, whizzing past Elspeth
and ending up stuck in the wall like a very
sparkly dagger.

"How dare you!" hissed Tatiana. "How
could you possibly think you'd get away
with this? Everyone knows how important
Daddy is. He'll speak to the authorities and
you'll all end up in jail!"

Elspeth trembled, but she looked straight at Tatiana. Things were moving too fast. Elspeth would have to think even faster. She looked over at Professor Bombast, but he was busy trying to stop the TV crews from broadcasting the chaos.

Elspeth grabbed Rory's hand. *There has to be a way out of this*, she thought. *What if—*

But before Elspeth could finish her thought, she heard a very cross voice coming from behind Tatiana.

"Not so fast," the voice squeaked threateningly.

Tatiana's head was jerked backwards. Esmerelda was standing behind her, clutching Tatiana's long blonde hair in one hand and a pair of scissors in the other.

"You're not the only one with scissors,

you know!" Esmerelda shrilled. "I know it was you who ruined my perfect hair!" She waved the scissors in the air. "I've realized that Tatiana is a nasty piece of work and that she's not my friend at all!"

"Nooooo! Not my beautiful hair! Anything but my hair!" Tatiana screeched, her face bright pink.

Elspeth turned around to see Tim Fitzgibbons hurrying towards her. He and his friends had tied up Miss Crabb and Gladys Goulash with a microphone cable, and Gladys was trying to gnaw through it.

"Elspeth, this is frightful!" Tim said breathlessly. He smoothed down his hair, looking anxious. "I'd never be able to get hold of my favourite shampoo in Outer Mongolia. It sounds like a hideous place! Now we've sorted out Crabb and Goulash, can you get us out of here?"

"What are we all waiting for?" cried Elspeth. She hauled at the front door with all her strength. "Let's get out of here and catch Tatiana's dad!"

The show-offs crowded round behind her, Esmerelda still holding Tatiana by her hair.

"You won't get out of that door, Elspeth," said Professor Bombast gravely. He marched towards them with a worried look on his face. "He's locked us in using Firensky Super-strength Glue." He scratched his head, making his curly black hair stick up even more than usual. "I'm afraid, old chaps, that we are TRAPPED!"

"OK. Let's go to the kitchens!" Elspeth whirled around, ready to lead everyone towards the kitchen exit.

But that was when they heard it. The rushing sound of lots and lots of water.

22

The Rushing Sound of Lots and Lots of Water

There was a simple explanation for the dreadful sound of rushing water. As you may remember, dear reader, Gladys Goulash had taken her annual bath that morning.

Gladys Goulash did not like washing. She found it a waste of time, and it went against her motto, which was: If Something Is a Lot of Effort, It's Not Worth Doing.

But once a year, just before the Look at Us! show, she took a soak, shaved all the black hairs off her hairy legs and trimmed her very long yellow toenails. That is what Gladys Goulash had done that morning.

Unfortunately there was so much black hair and so many toenail clippings that the bathtub had not drained. Gladys hadn't bothered checking the taps were off properly, either, and while the show-offs were performing, a LOT of water had filled up the bathroom.

It kept flowing. It flowed through the upstairs corridors. It snuck under doors and it ran down the stairs. Now there was a huge river of water rushing through the school, soaking the thick patterned rugs and the red velvet curtains. It raced towards Elspeth and Rory and Professor Bombast and the show-offs and, because the doors had been locked with Firensky Superstrength Glue, the water had nowhere to go. In just a few seconds it was up to their ankles and rising fast.

"The basement exit will already be flooded," yelled Professor Bombast above the noise of the rushing water. "We're stuck!" He pushed one of the cameramen out of his way. "Do stop filming, old chap! Can't you see this is an emergency?"

Elspeth shivered with fear. Rory looked like he might cry.

"It's OK. We can break out through a window!" squealed Esmerelda.

Esmerelda was an excellent gymnast, and she wasn't going to let a crisis get in the way of a showing-off opportunity. Before anyone could stop her, she took a run, did a splashy cartwheel, a round-off and jumped up towards one of the high pointy windows. She landed neatly on the windowsill and kicked out with the heel of her tap shoe, smashing the glass window.

"Come on, everyone," Tim shouted. "Form a human pyramid!"

The show-offs didn't have to be told twice. With a TV crew following their every move, they bent and jumped and climbed until there was a wall of bodies leading up to the window.

Esmerelda had handed Tatiana to another of the show-offs, who was clinging on to her. Nobody wanted Tatiana to get away with her awful tricks. And without Tatiana wriggling and kicking, the human pyramid worked perfectly.

"You first, Elspeth," Tim said encouragingly. "Step on Rory's back, then on the next person, just like it's a staircase. We'll get you out of here in no time."

Elspeth didn't stop to think twice. She'd never trusted any of these children, but things were changing. Things were changing faster than Gladys Goulash changed her slug soup recipe. She took a deep breath and climbed up.

"Sorry, Rory!" she said, taking the first step on to his back.

"No worries, Elspeth," came a muffled voice from the human pyramid.

Elspeth took three more wobbly steps, and then she pulled herself up to stand next to Esmerelda on the windowsill.

She steadied herself and took a look around. What she saw made her think she was dreaming.

There were hundreds of police officers all around the school. There were dozens of photographers, lots of flashing lights and another two TV crews. Ivan Firensky was struggling and kicking as two policemen put a pair of handcuffs on him. Lots of official people were taking statements. Elspeth slid down a drainpipe, jumped on to the grass and breathed in fresh air for the first time in a year. She was fine! No shrivelling up at all. Elspeth ran forward on the lawn, spun round and looked back at the school.

23

The Pandora Pants
School for Show-offs
from the Outside

Elspeth had only ever seen the Pandora
Pants School for Show-offs from the inside.
It looked just as horrible from the outside.
She stared at it for a long moment.

*I will never, ever, set foot in that place
again,* she promised herself.

The police had propped a ladder up
against the wall, and the show-offs were

clambering out of the window and down to safety. Some show-offs were taking the opportunity to display their jumping and cartwheeling skills, and doing backflips as soon as they landed on the grass.

Elspeth spotted the police climbing in through the window with another ladder, then saw Miss Crabb and Gladys Goulash being hauled out into the bright sunshine.

"Firensky, you festering old goat!" screamed Miss Crabb. "I thought you loved me. I'll get you for this!"

For a second, Elspeth felt sorry for Miss Crabb. Then she remembered being shouted at, having to wash filthy pots all day and being made to sleep in a wardrobe, and Elspeth didn't feel sorry for her AT ALL.

Elspeth saw Professor Bombast shuffling up to Madame Chi-chi, looking sheepish.

"Well, this is all rather out of the blue," he muttered. "With that Firensky chap behind bars I can make a fresh start. Madame Chi-chi, I don't suppose you'd care to, ahem … marry me? I thought you might like to help me run this place as a quiet school for quiet children."

There was a shriek of delight and Madame Chi-chi planted another big lipsticky kiss on Professor Bombast's cheek.

"Plus," said Professor Bombast wisely, "I will need an assistant in the school to look after Cutie-pie and wipe his little bottom, and I have chosen Tatiana Firensky. While her daddy is in jail she will be well looked after, provided she works hard."

There was a loud scream of horror from Tatiana. "Noooo!" she shouted. "Assistant? I can't be an ASSISTANT! Do you know how much my perfect fingernails are insured for, you stupid little man? Not to mention my beautiful hair!"

"Do shut up, Tatiana," called Ivan Firensky, as he was led into a police van. "It's all over. You're a spoilt brat and you'd better do as the man says."

Elspeth tried not to laugh as she caught a glimpse of Tatiana's disgusted face. But then she started getting the icy, worried feeling in her tummy again. Without a mum and dad to collect her, what should she do now? Would the police put her in a children's home? Or send her to live with one of the awful show-offs?

Elspeth turned around to look for Rory. She spotted him jumping up and down trying to find his parents, or at least his butler.

"Rory, I'm going to make a run for it,"

Elspeth said. "This is my chance to go home. But I can't risk waiting too long. I need to get to the nearest town."

Rory stopped jumping and went pale. "Elspeth, you'll never make it. It's miles and miles! Wait here with me. Maybe you could stay at my house for a bit. Now all this has been on TV, there's no way my parents will send me away to boarding school again!"

But Elspeth only had one thing on her mind. She had to get back home.

"Give me your address," she said quickly. "I'll write and tell you where I end up."

Rory pulled the pen out of his shirt pocket, then patted his trouser pockets in a panic. "My notebook got soaked in the flood. I don't have anything to write on!"

"Write it on my arm," Elspeth said. Out of the corner of her eye she could see a smiley police officer organizing children into groups. The police officer would be with them any second, and it would be obvious Elspeth didn't have anyone to collect her. "No, wait – my shoe! Write it on the white toe bit. Dad already drew all over the rest of them."

Rory scribbled his address on her shoe and stood up again quickly. They looked at each other and Elspeth felt like she might laugh and cry at the same time.

"Go, before they catch up with you," Rory said.

Elspeth hugged her only friend in the world. Then she turned around and started running as fast as she could.

24

In Fact, She Had Never Run So Fast in Her Life

Elspeth ran until she had no more breath in her. She ran until she felt sick and her hair was sticking to the back of her neck. When she turned around and looked at the school, it still didn't seem that far away. The road ahead was long and twisty. For the first time, Elspeth wondered if she had made a terrible mistake. She had no water or food,

no money. But all she could do was keep
on running.

Every so often a limo would pass her –
with the school on the news, all the parents
who hadn't been at the Look at Us! show
were sending chauffeurs to pick up their
precious show-offs.

Elspeth ducked into the bushes whenever
a car passed, but eventually a bright pink
Rolls Royce whizzed up behind her and
screeched to a halt before she had a chance
to hide. The window whirred down.

"Excuse me, miss," said a worried voice. A red-faced driver in a peaked cap peered at her. "I don't suppose you're Miss Tatiana Firensky, are you?"

Elspeth didn't even blink. "Why yes, I am!" she said smoothly. She tried to make her voice a bit squeakier than normal.

"Thank goodness!" said the driver. "I'm ever so sorry, miss. It's my first day on the job and your mother sent me down here. She said you like to have your own personal car. I was meant to be here sooner, but I got lost! I looked for you up at the school, but there's so many people running around…" He paused to take off his cap and wipe the sweat from his forehead. "Do get in please, miss. I hope you'll forgive me for being late."

Elspeth hopped in before she could lose her nerve.

So this is how the show-offs travel, she thought to herself. The back seat was covered in the softest white leather. There was a small ice box next to her full of cold fizzy drinks. And she had a TV screen in front of her with all the channels she could ever want to watch – all for her.

How am I going to get myself out of this before I end up at Tatiana's mansion? she thought. She tried to think of a clever plan, but her brain seemed to be stuck. Sometimes this happens to all of us, dear reader, when we are very worried about something.

The car sped away and Elspeth wondered what she had got herself into.

"One thing, miss," called the driver. "Your mother said we must stop off at Horrads. You can get a new fur coat, or anything else you fancy, and charge it to her account. Seeing as you've been doing so well at school. A treat."

"Um … that sounds super," Elspeth said eventually. "And –" Elspeth had a flash of inspiration – "then I shall need you to take me to Skipping Hopton."

"Skipping Hopton?" asked the driver. "That's a fair drive. Don't you want to go straight home, miss?"

Elspeth gave a tinkly laugh. "Don't be silly!" she said firmly. "Mummy and Daddy know I shall be spending the weekend in Skipping Hopton. With my … old nanny."

If Elspeth had learned one thing from the Pandora Pants School for Show-offs, it was that saying things in a confident voice meant people were more likely to believe you.

Four hours later, they finally arrived in Skipping Hopton. It was getting dark. Elspeth pressed her nose to the glass. She recognized the street that led to her old school and the park with the swings. As they drove through the village, more and more memories started coming back to her.

By the time the car pulled slowly into her street, Elspeth had never been so desperate to get out of a car in her life.

"Thank you ever so much, I'll just get out here," Elspeth said.

The driver looked worried, but shrugged. "If you're sure, miss," he said, tipping his cap at Elspeth as she opened the door.

Elspeth waited until the pink Rolls Royce had turned at the end of the street before she started running towards her front door.

25
In Front of Elspeth's Front Door

Elspeth stopped in dismay, staring at the sweet shop and the flat above it. It was dark. So dark she knew at once that nobody was home. Cobwebs stretched across the front door and the grass outside was long and messy. It looked like nobody had been there for some time. You can imagine, dear reader, how scary it is to feel all alone in the world.

And now, looking at the dark house, Elspeth felt more alone than ever.

Blinking back tears, Elspeth trudged up the steps to the front door. The spare key was in its usual place under a pot, and she let herself in. She flicked on the lights and walked through each room, trying not to panic. *Where are you?* she thought.

Then she saw the note.

Dear, dear Elspeth,

If you find this note, darling girl, you've made it home — that's wonderful. We know someone kidnapped you. We had a mysterious phone call from a woman who wouldn't give her name. She told us you've been stolen and taken to the other side of the world … but we are getting on a plane tonight. We will find you! Go straight to the police and ask them for help.

Mum and Dad xxx

All the fear rushed away, leaving Elspeth's legs feeling like jelly. Her mum and dad were alive! It was the most glorious feeling in the world. Elspeth jumped up and down on the sofa in delight, then she lay back and ate a slice of Horrads sponge cake for dinner.

Then she realized she'd better copy down Rory's address. After all, he was her only friend in the world and would be waiting to hear from her.

Elspeth took off her right trainer and copied out the address Rory had scribbled on the toe. Then she picked up the shoe again and looked at it more closely. In among the stars and swirls were lines of numbers, in tiny writing.

Hold on a minute, Elspeth thought. *This looks like a code!* She sat bolt upright again.

"This IS a code!" she said out loud. "That song is a list of ingredients and THIS is the code!" She started humming, and sure enough, every single word of the song came rushing back to her. "I can remember it all!"

Elspeth grabbed a sheet of paper and hummed and scribbled until she had the recipe all written down. She stared at the sheet of paper in awe. The Hart family Extra-special Sticky Toffee Sauce recipe. The one her parents were going to use to make their fortune. Elspeth hesitated. Would it be safe, written down like that? Then she remembered that Miss Crabb, Gladys Goulash and Ivan Firensky were in jail.

Elspeth flopped back on to the sofa and sighed in relief.

When Elspeth tucked herself up in bed that night, she opened the window wide so she could breathe in the lovely fresh air. She lay quietly in her favourite pyjamas, looking up at the glow-in-the-dark stars on her ceiling. The recipe was safe from Miss Crabb. Elspeth was safe from Miss Crabb. Her parents were alive. All Elspeth had to do now was find them.

I'm going to find you, Mum and Dad, Elspeth thought. *I'm going to find you and then we can all come home together.*

She fell into a proper deep sleep for the first time in a whole year. And for the first time in a year, Elspeth Hart couldn't wait for tomorrow.

26
But When
Tomorrow Arrived…

So that may seem like a very happy ending,
dear reader, but I am afraid that it is not
the end of the story. The very next day,
as Elspeth was hurrying to the police
station, she saw a huge black headline on a
newspaper stand outside the grocery shop.

Elspeth grabbed a copy and started
reading.

EVIL DINNER LADIES IN DARING ESCAPE!

A nationwide search has started after two dastardly dinner ladies, Miss Crabb and Gladys Goulash, escaped from the high-security Grimguts prison yesterday. It is thought that the dinner ladies, arrested only yesterday for a treacherous kidnapping and fraud plot, may have escaped by hiding in large bags of dirty laundry.

Members of the public are advised not to approach them, as they are highly dangerous and smell awful.

Elspeth stared at the newspaper in horror. It looked like her enemies were after her again already.

But that, dear reader, is a story for another day.

Hart's Extra-special Sticky Toffee Sauce

One is for sugar
Two is for butter
Three is for syrup
Four is for vanilla
Five is for treacle
Six is for cream

Melt it all in till it tastes like a dream!

1=55
2=55
3=1
6=200
5=1
4=0.5

You can find the Extra-special Sticky Toffee Sauce recipe
and much more on my website!
www.elspethhart.com

Sarah
Forbes

Sarah was born in Aberdeen and
currently lives in Edinburgh. She used to
work on magazines, interviewing pop stars
for a living, but now she works as an editor,
helping other writers to create their own
stories. *Elspeth Hart and the School for
Show-offs* is Sarah's debut novel.